Clint Faraday
book 31
Rest in Pieces

Clint is talking with friends in a little bar in Puerto Armuelles when an obnoxious tourist makes a pass at Tyna. He removes him from the bar, not gently.

Julio, a friend, says that one will likely end up with R.I.P. on his headstone – for rest in pieces.

Two days later the man is found in his boat – chopped to pieces.

Contents

About the author

CD Moulton has traveled extensively over much of the world both in the music business, where he was a rock guitarist, songwriter and arranger and in an import/export business. He has been everything from a bar owner to auto salvage (junkyard) manager, longshoreman to high steel worker, orchid grower to landscaper, tropical fish farmer to commercial fisherman. He started writing books in 1983 and has published more than 350 books as of January 1, 2023. His most popular books to date are about research with orchids, though much of his science fiction and fantasy work has proven popular. He wrote the CD Grimes, PI series, and the Det. Nick Storie series, Clint Faraday series, and many other works.

He now resides in Gualaca, Chiriqui, Panamá, where he writes books, plays music with friends, does research with orchids and medicinal plants. He has lately become involved in fighting for the rights of the indigenous people, who are among his closest friends, and in fighting the extreme corruption in the courts and police in Panamá.

He offers the free e-book, *Fading Paradise*, that explains what he has been through because of the corruption.

CD is the discoverer of the Chadam Protocol for curing cancer.

Facebook page Ambrosia peruviana for cancer.

Rest in Pieces

The Obnoxious Tourist

Clint Faraday, retired PI from Florida, laughed at the story Julio Santos had told about a gringo who used Spanish to say something that came out very differently from what the speaker had intended. Tyna, Clint's beautiful young wife, said they should hear what some tourists, even Panameños, said when they tried to speak the Indio dialect.

"The gringo tangle," Clint agreed. "When I was learning Spanish, in Bocas, I was living in a two story house with a balcony over the street. I was there, watching people pass one morning. It was drizzling rain, and I would call, 'Poco mojada!' I kept getting weird looks and didn't know why."

Julio and Tyna laughed. George E. Harris, a somewhat crude tourist from Missouri, in the states, asked what the hell that was supposed to mean.

"Mojado means wet or damp, mojada is a short woman," Julio explained. "He was saying 'Little short woman!' to short women. They thought he was insulting them."

"Why do you people always make sick jokes about us people from the US? After all, we come here and spend our money! Why make fun of us because we don't speak Spanish? That's what's insulting!" He was getting red in the face.

"In case it slipped by your acute mind, I was a gringo, so why would I insult myself? It's just something that happens when you're learning any language. Don't get your shorts in a knot," Clint said.

Harris stared and shrugged. He yelled, "Girlie! Bring me another rum and Coke!"

Lisa came to the table. "Que?"

"Un otro ron con Coca Cola," Julio said.

"Why the hell don't you people learn English, if you want us to come spend our money here?" Harris spat.

"Because the language here is Spanish. If I go to the US, I will learn English," Julio said.

"You're already speaking pretty good English," Harris replied. "I wasn't talking about you!"

"Let's see. They should learn English if they want you to come spend your money here," Clint said. "The fact that they don't see ten people who speak English here in a month, eight of whom speak enough Spanish to order a rum and Coke, doesn't figure into it.

"Tell me something. If any of these people go to

wherever you're from and into a bar, should the bartender and waitress there speak Spanish because they're spending their money there?" Clint asked.

"You're an asshole!" Harris said.

"Me? Right! Then why don't you answer? Is it because you're such a big bad important hotshit everyone everywhere should change their life to accommodate you?

"There's definitely an asshole here. Why don't we take a vote to see who it is? The whole bar can vote!"

Harris got up and stomped over to the bar, mumbling. The two men standing at the bar moved away when he came. He didn't seem to notice.

People would come in and come to the table to chat a bit with Clint and his wife. A couple of them went to the bar to order. Harris tried to talk to them, but they didn't speak English. Harris said, a bit loudly, "You go talk to that Clint guy, but you don't speak any English whenever I say something! You're assholes!"

Julio went to say, "Clint was speaking English to you because he is a considerate and polite kind of person. He speaks better Spanish than I do. He speaks the dialect as well as I do.

"Maybe we should take the vote, like Clint

suggested, about who's the asshole, asshole!"

"You better get out of my face before I *get* you out of it!"

"Give it your best shot, bigshit!"

"Tranquilo!" the bartender demanded sternly. "Calmarse o salir!" (Calm down. Calm down or leave.)

Julio apologized and went back to the table.

They talked awhile and Tyna went to the baño. She was coming back and walked past Harris, who suddenly grabbed her arm and said something. Clint was on his feet and half-way there when she used the knee to the crotch Clint taught her. Harris squealed and doubled over. Clint caught him by the back of his shirt and his belt and threw him out into the street.

"You ever put a hand on my wife again and I'm going to beat you to death! Got it?!"

Harris groaned and mumbled something about his Colombian friends. Clint grabbed him by the hair and snarled, "What did you say?"

"Nothing! I had too much to drink! I didn't say nothing!"

Clint bounced his head off the pavement and went back inside. He was so mad he could bite through a twenty penny nail. He had to stop himself from beating the asshole to death, right then.

He took a few deep breaths and sat at the table.

"I almost went over the edge on that one," he said.

"That one is going to end up with a headstone that says R.I.P. – for rest in pieces," Julio said. "How in hell has he managed to live this long? I wonder!"

"He's so big he intimidates people," Lisa said. "He grabbed at me and I told him he was ten seconds from getting his balls cut off!"

They chatted awhile, then Clint said it was time to get back to the house, where his friends were watching his eight months old child. It had been a very good night, except for the one unpleasant incident.

Clint, Tyna and Nito stayed at Rafaela's place for two more days before anything else untoward happened. Several gringos asked him why he was staying in the poorer section of town with the Indios, instead of at the hotel. He explained that he was an Indio (he was honored to be the second white person to ever be declared a Ngobe by the councils on the comarcas) and his wife was an India. He was going to raise his son in the Indio tradition. His son was not going to turn out to be like far too many of the non-Indio children.

They would return to David the following day,

then to Soloy and into the comarca to Quebrada Tula. This afternoon was to be spent with their friends.

Clint's cellular buzzed and he looked at the caller ID. Esteban, from the Policía Nacionál?

"Clint Faraday here. Hi, Esteban. Que paso?"

"Hello, Clint. I have lately been transferred to Puerto Armuelles to head the violent crimes. I understand that you had a serious confrontation with a George Evan Harris three nights ago?"

"Harris? Oh, the asshole gringo from Missouri. Yeah."

"He has been found dead in his boat by the river. I need any information you may have."

"I don't know anything about him. I met him in the bar and did *not* like him.

"Dead? How?"

"It is as bloody a mess as I have ever seen. He was chopped up with a machete, I think. His arms are cut off and one leg – and his head is barely still attached."

"Rest in pieces. It fits."

"What?"

"Something a friend said about him. His head-stone would read R.I.P. For rest in pieces."

"It's quite accurate a description, anyhow. Will you help with this one? I have only been here two days and don't know the people. You do."

"We were going back to Tula, but I can spend a few days on it here. Rafaela's going with us, so she and Tyna can go on. I'll see if I can dig anything up."

Clint looked at the pictures. The boat was a bloody mess of arms and a leg in the left side rear and the rest of the body in the front, ahead of the console. There were cuts all over the body, but Doc had said he wasn't tortured, as such. Someone started cutting him and had gone into a frenzy. There was a lot of emotion behind this one.

Clint thought for a minute. He wasn't sure he wanted to get involved on a case where some idiot asshole who constantly asked for it finally got it. Harris probably came across a native Panamanian out there and felt his big fancy boat meant he had the right to swamp the smaller craft or cayucas (though it would be next to impossible to swamp a cayuca without coming very close to hitting it). He probably stopped to be insulting and obnoxious to someone who answered the challenge in exactly the way he could expect, if he wasn't such an idiot.

He remembered something, and Esteban was a friend.

"I'll see what I can find. I'll get in touch if

there's anything beyond the fact he was an obnoxious asshole idiot bastard who thought we Panamanians should bow and scrape to his royal rusty ass.

"You may gather I don't care if someone cut him up and couldn't care less if it was a torture killing.

"You say his boat? He came in it or bought it here? What kind was it?"

"A two thousand ten Harborcraft twenty two footer he bought in Nicaragua, went to Costa Rica, where he was not welcomed past the first ten minutes after arrival, then came around to Puerto Armuelles, where you noted the reception he was enjoying. He arrived the day before your meeting with him and was staying at a place owned by Samuél Costas. You possibly know the place. Between the wharf and Punta Piedra. Costas says he didn't know him well, that a cousin in Costa Rica arranged for him to stay there."

"I think I know Sam Costas. I can get Tyna, Rafael and Nito on their way and go out to see him. He lives just out of town? That place with the long dock that sits fifteen feet above the water at low tide?"

"Yes. Thanks, Clint."

Clint rang off and thought for a minute or two, then went to tell Tyna the news. She shook her head and asked him if it was worth the trouble to find the killer of someone who should have been cut to pieces twenty years ago.

"It's for Esteban. Harris? Big deal! Unsolvable! No evidence!"

"We agree on everything, Love. Don't be away too long."

Clint went into town and to the Costas house. Sam was sitting on the rear porch with a cup of coffee. He offered Clint some. It was a special coffee he got in a place he wouldn't tell anyone else about. Clint agreed that he was also a coffee addict and took a cup. He tasted it.

"Ah! The Enel Fortuna dam! I already get my coffee at home there, except when we're on the comarca, where there's some very much like it."

"What part of the comarca?"

"Between Soloy and Quebrada Tula. I won't tell you any closer."

"Above Boca de Balsa. That's where this came from. Good to know about the dam, though. I'd heard there was good coffee there."

They chatted a few minutes about the comarca. Sam had cousins who were Ngobe. He knew that Clint was a declared Ngobe. Finally, Clint said, "What about that Harris asshole? That's why I'm here."

"Yes. I was waiting for you to ask. I know very little about him, except that my cousin, Arturo

Morales, in San José, sent him here. I did not much like him, at first, but learned to despise him, very soon. I should have known that anyone Arturo sent would be a bad person."

"Ah! Arturo is into drugs?"

"No. He says that's too hot an issue, right now. He's into something else crooked. Colombians and Venezuelans."

"With Colombians *and* Venezuelans? That's not quite everyday! It's usually Colombians *or* Venezuelans!"

"So I have been led to believe, but there was a Colombian and two Venezuelans here to meet with him. They went down by the dock, where they couldn't be heard. I didn't like any of them. They all were trying to look like Che Guevara.

"I have nothing against Che Guevara, but I do have a lot against his would-be copiers. None of them are like he was."

"You don't know what they're into?"

"No. I don't want to know."

"I don't blame you."

Clint went back into town and to the police station to talk with Esteban, half an hour later. He asked about the Colombians and Venezuelans. Esteban didn't know anything about them. He had seen a man who might be one of them on the street the day before. He would find out what there was to know about them. He called in a woman, Gilda Ramos, who had been on the police force in Puerto Armuelles for several years as aide to the chief, of sorts. Esteban asked her about the three foreigners.

"I saw one they call Tonio at the China across from the Banco HSBC. The other two, I think, are near Provenir. Do you want me to have them checked?"

"I want to know who, where, when, why and how about them."

"Probably a couple of hours – Panameño."

"An hour Panameño" is a standing joke in the country. A hour Panameño was anywhere from two hours to four days. "An hour – Gringo" is an hour, by the clock. While one o'clock Panameño is as much as meaningless, one o'clock gringo is one o'clock.

She went out. Esteban said it was lunch time, so they went to Yola's for a good meal. Clint went to look over the murder boat after lunch, then they went back to the station. Gilda said she had some information about Antonio Vega, the Colombian. He was someone they had little information about in any records she could find. He was an importer of many things in Bogota, Cali and Medellin. She had him stopped for an ID check when he went to three banks in the period of less than one hour (gringo!). That was a suspicious circumstance. He had said he was trying to get pesos changed into Balboas, but none of them would change money. She told him he had to go to Frontera, Colón or Panamá City for exchanging foreign money.

"I have an enquiry sent to Bogota about him. They haven't answered, so I am suspicious."

"Suspicious? Why?" Clint asked.

"If he was a regular businessman, they would answer very quickly. If they have him under suspicion for any reason, they will wait. If he is working for the government there, or for that of the Estados, they will not have information about him, but will contact me to learn what he is doing that we know about. It is a political game they play. I become very suspicious of anyone who tries to look like Castro or Guevara. Castro and Guevara were sincere in their beliefs, even if we don't agree with them. The copiers are more usually wanting only to grab power for them-selves by their pretending to care about the people."

"Yes. They start little guerilla wars," Esteban added. "Perhaps we should find what Vega is importing?"

"I think we should also check out Harris, very carefully," Clint suggested. "I'll want to know what he was into. His personality type suggests something to me. I think I know just what kind of thing he would be into. I just wonder what they found out about him or what he tried to pull.”

“Pull?” from Gilda.

“It’s an expression. What he was trying to ... scam them out of.”

“Scam? Oh, yes! Defraud.”

“Whatever, that boat would have carried very little in bulky material. It would carry a lot of cash. Possibly that counterfeit from Colombia that is so good and very hard to detect?” Esteban suggested. “It would not be drugs. The boats are checked for drugs in too many ways.”

“It could be, but I’m thinking of something else,” Clint replied. “I’ll check with friends in the states. You can concentrate on finding out what the Venezuelans are up to and what their connections with Vega are about.”

They talked about the case a bit more, then Clint headed back to Rafael’s house. He would stay there, while in Puerto Armuelles. He used his computer to check on Harris in Missouri. He was from outside of Joplin, was not popular there, though not nearly to the degree he was elsewhere. He was big into paramilitary groups, which is what Clint suspected. He had some connections, but not anything big enough to worry about. Most definitely not enough to cause him to be investigated by the government for anything past unpaid taxes. That was minor. He had been fined a hundred dollars for not reporting income of less than five thousand dollars once. He had a weapons charge against him that was dropped. An automatic rifle that was iffy. He might have bought it innocently.

Yeah, right! He did anything innocently!

One thing did come across. He tended to brag about contacts and deals that he wasn't involved in directly as though he was important to them. He had claimed to be a close relative of the senator of that name, but it turned out he was, if at all, a distant cousin who had never met the senator. He claimed to be close to a semi-mafia character named Giovanni. It turned out he had spoken to him once in a restaurant.

The way Clint was putting this together, Harris had made claims that he could get financial aid or weapons or such for a second-rate guerilla operation in Colombia or Venezuela, they came to meet him, learned he was all bullshit, and had gone into a fury about it. Exit Harris. R.I.P.

Clint sat back. There was something missing.

That was an understatement!

Clint decided the next step would be to find out what Arturo Morales was up to. That should give him a more solid connection.

Esteban called to say Gilda had a lot of new information coming in that didn't seem to make much sense. Clint said he'd be there in a few minutes. He finished his e-mail and shut down the computer, then headed for the station.

"The Venezuelans are Miguel Abrego L. and Frederico Narez C.," Gilda reported. "They are supposedly here to investigate the oil pipeline to Chiriqui Grande, but they haven't been anywhere near the terminal here and have never been to Chiriqui Grande. They are here because they want to establish a Pacific port where they can bring in Venezuelan cedar. They are here because they want to establish bank accounts in this country to be able to deal with the Estados in importing automobile parts and exporting clothing made in Venezuela. They are here as tourists. They are here to investigate buying copper. They are here for many reasons, none of which are true. That means they are here for illegal activity."

"They're half-assed amateurs who were dealing with half-assed amateurs," Clint agreed. "Any professional crook would have one solid story and would stick to it.

"What was the connection with Vega?"

"Vega is a tourist who is here looking for investment opportunity. He is here to establish banking connections. That is the one thing that does not conflict with what the Venezuelans say. Perhaps that is a real connection. It is a thing that was in all of their stories."

"What you call Freudian," Esteban said. "Now we have to find what the banking connection connects."

"They will want to move a lot of money," Clint mused. "It isn't laundering. They would be in the city or maybe Colón for that, certainly not here in Puerto Armuelles. I think whatever they're into is something to be transferred from one to the other here, where no one would be looking for whatever it is. Funny money ain't it. That means it's, probably, anyhow, weapons for a guerilla action that would end up with a lot of innocent people getting killed and nothing else accomplished.

"First we have to trace and put a stop to it, here. Maybe four more schemers can rest in pieces as a message to keep out of Puerto Armuelles."

"Four more? Vegas, Narez, Abrego and who?"

Esteban asked.

"A distant cousin," Clint replied. "Someone who set the whole deal up. I wonder if he's the only legit crook in it or if he's just another amateur wannabe."

Gilda looked questioning, Esteban thoughtful. Esteban suddenly said, "Someone brought them together! You know who!"

"I *think* I know who," Clint cautioned. "I've *thought* I had answers to a lot of things that weren't answers."

"Yes. I know of a couple of those. We were both out in the left field when the ball was hit to the right field."

"You're getting better," Clint said.

"What?"

"Just 'Out in left field' is enough."

"Oh." Clint got the finger. Gilda laughed. "So let's get into whatever field is the proper one," she suggested. They all had to agree with that!

"Well, I wonder if I'm going to have to go to San José? I *hate* San José!" Clint protested. "Oh, well. What the hell!"

"You hate it? Why?" Gilda asked.

"I used to like it. Now, you can't go out at night without getting mugged, or worse. It's become a jungle, like some cities in the states. It's worse than Colón – and Colón is bad!"

"So I've heard. I'll give you police passes. We have the agreements with Costa Rica," Esteban said.

"I didn't say I was going!"

"You wouldn't have even brought it up if you weren't."

That got Esteban the finger.

Clint went to Rafael's and packed a few things. One day in Costa Rica should do it, so it would probably take a week, plus. He checked to be sure things were secure and that he had all the information he needed, then caught a bus to Frontera and then to San José. He checked into the Sunshine Hotel (Brother!) and looked in the directory for Arturo Morales. There were six of them. He called each to ask if he was the cousin of Samuél Costas. The fourth was.

"I have to talk with you about Colombia and Venezuela," Clint said.

"Colombia? Venezuela? I don't know anything about Colombia or Venezuela!"

"Harris, Abrego, Vega, Narez?"

He hung up. Clint grinned. The address was in the directory.

It was getting dark. It would have to wait until tomorrow.

The taxi let Clint out in front of the address,

which was an almacen. He said he would wait, if Clint liked. This wasn't a good section of the city.

"There's a good section?" Clint asked, with a grin.

"Sadly, not anymore." Clint waved and he drove off. Clint went into the little shop and nodded at the man in the caja. A caja with steel bars across the little window. There was a steel entrance door that opened with a buzzer from inside the caja. If anyone tried to hold him up or steal something, they couldn't get back out without him unlocking the electric lock. He did a little something as he went in

Lovely town. Clint remembered when, a very short time ago, this was a good city to visit.

President Martinelli, take a good long look! he thought.

"Arturo?"

"Yeah. What?"

"I'm Clint Faraday. I called yesterday afternoon about Colombia and Venezuela."

"Good for you."

"You'd better wise up, pal! As Harris learned, dealing with half-assed idiot amateurs can be dangerous, especially when you're another idiot half-assed amateur!"

"You have a point, but I have the advantage here. You can get back out if I let you out. You wouldn't be the first to come in here and never leave."

"Yes, I would. It looks like you'd have learned from this that running your mouth about how big and bad you are usually ends up with you being cut bait. I can leave anytime I like, if you're laying in there, dead, or if you're sitting there watching me."

He looked wary. "Oh? Why not walk out right now?"

Clint went to the door and pulled it open, then turned back to raise an eyebrow at a suddenly sweating Arturo Morales.

"What..!? How..!?"

"I'm not a wannabe amateur. I want a couple of answers and you're going to give them to me, capiche?"

"I can call the police with a button! You can't get away!"

Clint took the papers that said he was working with the police in Puerto Armuelles. His hand was over the "Puerto Armuelles, Chiriqui, Panamá" line.

"Give it a go! *I'm* the police! If you're here, dead, I just happened to walk in and find you like that! I pushed the buzzer to call my fellow officers. You know how that works!"

"You couldn't push the buzzer from out there!"

He was really sweating now.

"Which they wouldn't notice."

"What do you want?"

"Who, what."

"A group. A man named Mike Abrego, a half-gringo, I think, wanted me to introduce someone who could get some things for them. I introduced George Harris, who I talked to a few times, to Abrego – for a hundred dollars American. That's all I know. I swear!"

"You just happened to know an American arms dealer? Really?"

"All I know is that he said he had connections and could get anything anyone wanted. I don't know if weapons was what they wanted. I didn't ask."

"Okay, for now. Put a contact light on the door to show you if someone knows how to make the catch not go into the slot." He walked out, taking the little metal disk with the glue patch on one side in the door catch with him.

He lucked out on this one! He could head right back to Puerto Armuelles. He could be there in six hours, time for dinner!

He wouldn't go to El Critico. It was a good restaurant, bar and brothel. He didn't go to those places, since he got married. – On the other hand, it was a really good bar and restaurant. The brothel part wasn't automatic. He might just accidentally run into one or two or three people there who were trying to look like Che Guevara! Tyna wouldn't care. She knew full well there was no competition there or anywhere else who could hold up for ten seconds.

He headed for the bus.

"Morales didn't have more connection than that. He won't let this kind of thing get in the way again. He's learned not to get involved with those people, I think. He could have faked being scared shitless, in most ways, but I doubt he can turn pasty pale and sweat like a pig by acting."

"But you learned they are trying to purchase armaments," Esteban replied. "That is what you suspected. I, also."

"I'm going to try to accidentally run into our wannabe trio tonight. I can suppose they go to El Critico?"

He called Gilda. She said they went there some nights. It was Friday, so a good bet one or more would be there. They didn't meet very often and seemed to be strangers when they did. They had that part down pretty good. If the man hadn't been looking for it, he wouldn't have seen the slip of paper that was in Abrego's hand when he shook hands with Vega or that the paper was in Vega's hand when they parted. Abrego had gone around a corner and stopped. Vega went into a restaurant, where he made a phone call. Abrego just happened to receive a call at that exact moment! What a *coincidence*!

Clint snickered at Gilda, who giggled. She didn't have much more, so they rang off.

Clint went to Rafaela's to find someone had tried to get in, but he'd put some security items in that made them sorry they tried – such as the automatic pepper spray if anyone tried to jimmy the back door and the camera that recorded the whole thing. Clint recognized the one trying to get in. He'd seen him on the street several times.

Clint cleaned up, replaced the pepper sprayer, and headed for El Critico. The place was just getting started at seven forty five. He got a table to one side, where he could see the entrance clearly, and ordered the corvina with papas fritas and a green salad. He enjoyed the meal and talked with a couple of the girls who worked there. They knew he wasn't looking for more than conversation.

One of the trio came in at eight twenty and went to the bar. Alfonso, the bartender, came to take his order, which he ordered, quite loudly, "Cuba Libre!"

"Never was," Alfonso replied, and made the rum

and Coke with a twist for him.

The guy said his name was Miguel. He was here from Colombia.

"Colombia?" Alfonso replied. "You speak more like Venezuela." He went to wait on another. Abrego looked around and turned to try to talk with one of the girls, who was coldly cordial to him. After about ten minutes of being basically ignored, he looked around the room again. When he spotted Clint sitting alone at the table, the only solo table at the time, he put his hands out, palms up. Clint shook his head and shrugged. Abrego came and asked if he could join him. He waved at the seat across.

"I'm Miguel, called Mike, seeing you're a gringo. My mother was a gringo."

"Clint. I'm Ngobe."

"Aren't ... aren't the Ngobe Indigenos?"

"Yes. My wife is Ngobe." He wouldn't know that didn't make any difference. The fact was, he was declared Ngobe by the council. Abrego nodded.

"I don't know why the putas won't even talk to me," he complained.

"Because they're used to the ones who try so hard to look like Che Guevara and know it will probably be a boring and not profitable night."

He didn't react much. He said he thought

Panamanians liked Che.

"Yes. He had principles, I guess. He resonated with the poorer people, who are most of these Latin countries. They didn't necessarily agree with everything, but they understood it."

"But why ... I mean, why is that negative for me?"

"Che, it was real. You are a copy of the real thing, so are false. That's how they look at it. A copy of a legal paper has no status here."

He looked thoughtful. "Well, that's not the way it is at home."

"You're not at home. There are any number of things that are looked at differently, here. This is a unique kind of country, in some ways."

"I was thinking of investing in a business here. It would not be a good idea?"

"Bocas del Toro, Isla Colón, you might do okay with the tourists who've had a bellyful of the US or England or so forth."

"We have to get the imperialist pigs out of Colombia!" he cried, a bit loudly.

"Oh, get real!" Clint fired back. "You aren't Colombian and that line lost it's impact with Nicaragua. When Ortega got the election, he was tossed out on his phony ass after a short time. Communism has no incentives, so won't work, Charlie!"

"He's president again!"

"And he's learned his hard lesson about world politics. What's your point?"

He stared at the table top for awhile. "I'm what the English call 'redundant,' aren't I?" he finally asked.

"That's about it. You need a new line, if you're going to get into any position of real power, then the really big guys will slap you down in a heartbeat if you don't follow their line. You'll just become another one of their puppets, dancing on their strings."

"I might have a new slant."

"You and half a million others. A new slant would mean a new approach. You can't come up with one. The last truly serious attempt was with computers, but that was thwarted, fast!

"There are too many people in the world. That means opportunity is there in an inverse ratio. If you can think of something, a few thousand have already thought of it. The only thing that will work is a personal freedom you can't get through these silly intrigues."

"Nicaragua proved for all time that you *can* do something! Those modern military sciences are useless in the jungles!"

"What? You missed it? I just *said* that Ortega proved you can get the power with that shit. You can't *hold* it! The only people who can use the method successfully are the Indigenos, who've lived in those jungles a few thousand years. You manage to get a lot of them killed with this shit and they don't forget it. Ever! It comes back to the simple fact that they can use the same thing against you and the cycle becomes never-ending. It's just plain stupid!"

"We'll see!"

"Yes, we will, won't we?"

Clint stayed there for awhile, but none of the others came in. Abrego had left as soon as Clint faced him down about his guerilla war dreams.

Clint remembered a little thing from a case awhile back and wondered. There was something that would work, but it would work by bringing total chaos, worldwide. Only those Indigenos in various places would survive in any real fashion. Most so-called civilized places couldn't. The people behind the present system, who thought they had protection, would be the first to go. The fact that human psychology would dictate what would happen ... better to think in different lines. He wouldn't be much affected. He was Ngobe and would be with the Ngobe. They wouldn't even noticeably be affected by the total demise of "civilization's" trappings.

He went back to Rafaela's place and sacked out. Saturday might be a better time to meet and feel out this bunch.

He had to find the real heads of this. It smelled to him. Who was using these suggestible morons in another tired plot – and why?

Clint had some experience with the type who would do this. He didn't think any of them he knew would be so stupid as to use amateurs that low on the scale.

Unless the object was for them to be caught? Why?

It was politics, but from several angles. Each facet was trying to use the others. That meant a manipulator who was good at it.

That also meant he would have to question the final finding. It might not be final.

Too tired to think straight. Goodnight, Clint Faraday! Hasta mañana!

The day dawned beautifully. The sunrise was colorful from the clouds just above the horizon to the east.

Clint drank three cups of coffee and had some papaya and pineapple. It was early enough that very few people would be on the streets, except those going to work.

He went out and walked the eight blocks into downtown. He went to the bus terminal and into the little restaurant there for more coffee and a couple hojaldres. He talked with a few people waiting to take the bus to David. They all agreed it was probably smarter to stay there, but what the hell?

The bus came in from David and four gringos got off and were wandering around. Clint asked where they were from. Two were from Modesto, California, and two from Carlson, Minnesota. They heard the view was fantastic, with which they agreed, and that things were relatively cheap here. But they didn't see any hotels or anything like that. Clint told them about the hostel and pointed to it. They would check in, then spend the day looking around the place. They knew a day was enough to just see the area, but that it was well worth seeing.

Clint headed toward the wharf and saw a familiar face. He went to him and said, "How're the eyes today, Mono?"

Mono means monkey. It was his nickname.

"That was a mean trap, Clint. I couldn't see for four hours and my eyes still burn."

"So? Don't fuck with me or my friends and it won't happen.

"On your own or a paid excursion?"

"Yeah. I could get some from them and could sell your computer for some."

"The computer won't work if you don't know a few things about it. It has a GPS sender and we can find it within one meter anytime we like.

"The Colombian or the Venezuelans?"

"No. Panamanian."

"Anyone I know?"

"No, I don't think so. She's from Veraguas."

"Adela?"

"No. Dona ... I'll be damned! You did it! It worked! You didn't have a clue, now you know her name's Dona and that she's from Veraguas.

"I didn't say anything, okay?"

Clint nodded and walked away. He knew her name was not Dona and that she might be from anywhere except Veraguas. Mono wasn't a good liar. When he lied, he looked a little too intently at you to see if you knew he was lying.

She wouldn't be from Puerto Armuelles. When Clint first asked, Mono hadn't considered his position and was telling the truth. It would be a woman. She would have been there long enough to know how to find Mono. That would probably mean a regular visitor, probably with relatives here. (See how a detective's mind works?) He could think of one it might be. He grabbed a taxi and went a little out of town. He went to a little roadside vendor and engaged in a little idle chatter while he drank a nance chicha.

"It's been nice weather lately," he said to Junio, the vendor. "I guess Sam's visitors have enjoyed this visit."

"Well, there's just that Sara woman, so far as I know. His wife's sister."

"Oh. I thought he said his cousin from Costa Rica was coming."

"He didn't stay two hours! Sam doesn't like him!"

"No, but Sara does."

"I don't know. She didn't seem to get along with him. She was yelling at him about something from Colombia or something. He went away right after."

"Weird family. Some of them always fighting others."

"Lots of families like that, but not so much as them."

"True. Well, I guess I'll go on back. If Arturo isn't here, there's no reason for me to be."

"Arturo?"

"From Costa Rica."

"Oh. It wasn't him. It was Donzo."

"Oh. Another relative to argue with," Clint said, with a laugh. Junio agreed.

Clint went back into town and to the police station to discuss the latest news with Esteban. He would have to learn who the Donzo character was. There were more in this than he'd thought, apparently. How many others from Costa Rica?

"I think I know the Donzo character," Esteban said. "He gets drunk and starts trouble. He gets braver and braver with each shot of seco. Wants to challenge anyone smaller than him. A couple have knocked him on his ass, but the type never learns. You once told that Frank person he had an alligator mouth and gecko ass. That fits him. He's another one who knows every bigshot and his dog, to hear him, but doesn't even recognize them in the same room. Makes you want to puke. Not bad, when sober. Can't handle the booze."

Clint nodded and said there seemed to be a lot of the type around lately.

"I guess I'll have to see what I can dig up about him. And about Sara."

"Sara Bailleras? She's a sister of the wife of Costas. She's a little imperious, but not a bad person, I think. She has problems with others in the family. The family seems to have problems with each other all the time. They get along with everyone not in the family, except a couple of them, when they're drunk."

"Don't be too sure. She hired Mono to steal my computer."

"According to Mono. I could tell you some things about that one!"

"No. Mono as much as said it wasn't her."

"Then it was."

"Okay. This is supposedly about some guns. A group of wannabe dictators want to start a little revolution with guerilla warfare and take over

Colombia and Venezuela. They're being used. The plan's totally silly. The trouble being, they would kill a bunch of the Indigenos in Colombia and Venezuela and start a thing that would go on for years. It's the kind of thing the CIA would instigate, but they're not involved, I think. It's not quite their kind of thing. I think the ones behind it will try to make it look like that, if anyone's caught. Protect their own asses.

"We have to find the top dogs and put an end to it. There's enough shit in the world without this."

"It's a matter of our ... Clint, the Colombian and the Venezuelans are the key to finding whoever's higher. You've already used that to get to here. There has to be a way to go on. They're still key. We're as much as in check, right now."

"Yes. I have to meet the others. I think I made Abrego think enough that he'll get very wary of them. I think he's slowly beginning to realize he's being used and that none of it's for him."

Esteban nodded. It was all too possible. "We have to find a way to get further into this. At the moment, we have too many moves that will put us where we are right now. In check. We have to be able to at least make it checkmate."

"That, you have right!"

Clint looked out over the water from the wharf. He saw Abrego and another like him walking out there and followed. They wouldn't know they were seen. Maybe Abrego would want to talk.

It took about fifteen minutes with him talking with some friends who spent a lot of time fishing from the wharf before Abrego saw him and came over to introduce Frederico Narez. People call him Rico.

"It's a great day for fishing. Yesterday, one of the people caught a yellowfin tuna that had to weigh a hundred pounds!" Narez said. "We were hoping to see someone catch something like that today."

Clint nodded. "When they're running, they catch some big ones. I saw them catch one that weighed a hundred eighty pounds a month or so ago. It took four of them to get it up here."

"We also wanted to talk where others would be out of range of this," Abrego said, taking a small button broadcast bug from his pocket. Clint took it and studied it carefully, then shook his head. "It's only a locator. It works like the one in my computer. It's through the GPS and can tell whoever where you are within one meter, anywhere on the planet. It doesn't broadcast sound, though it's possible there's something such on you. Is there evidence of that?"

"I found this by accident. It was in a medallion on a key chain I always carried and I dropped it on the cement. This came loose. I've checked everything else where this kind of thing can be and didn't find anything. A few times, people seemed to know what I'd said to someone else when no one was around but us."

"So. You see what's happening?" Clint asked.

"Somebody's making us do the work so they can be boss, right?" Narez asked.

"Something like that. You can turn it around on them, but you'd better be aware that this kind of thing can't work anymore."

"Miguel explained that someone told him some things he couldn't refute or deny about it, about Nicaragua and how that proved for all time that these things can't work, except in the jungle, then they turn it back on you the way you turned it on someone else."

"Exactly."

"Then it is hopeless that we can ever be free?"

"You didn't want anybody to be free. You just wanted them to be slaves to you instead of the way it is now, with all of you being slaves to whoever's running things wherever you are. It won't work. They've managed to become too powerful. I think it's slowly dawning on the idiots that they're going to die, just like everyone else, and it's all for nothing, in the long run. They stop advance of the race, but it doesn't matter. All that matters is a sense of power for them. It's an empty thing."

"Indio philosophy."

"But it's true."

"A lot of it is. Too much, really. We're dogs chasing our tails and don't know how to stop. We're dizzy from it."

"That's pretty good philosophy, on its own," Clint said. "Want to turn this back on them? Remember; they've been using you in their own scheme to the point you're now expendable. You know too much that can turn back on them. Ask Harris or Noriega how they handle those things.

"Did one of you do that? You should get a medal!"

"I wanted to, a couple of times, when I learned he was a pile of horseshit!" Abrego spat. "He knew every big arms dealer in Israel, Russia, Syria and the US. He didn't know his own Aunt Suzie! Total horseshit! We came here to make a deal and ended up in trouble from both ends!"

See if he could hit something! It was now a good time – if he was right!

"Sara and Donzo, and you're in the middle?"

"So. You know it all and you were using us in your own way."

"No. I was guessing and adding things. You confirmed it.

"Esteban, a friend, was using chess terms to describe it. This was a Queen's Gambit, with you as pawns. A pawn can capture a queen."

"We have to consider one other. We have to know which side he's on," Narez warned.

"Vega? I can't quite figure that. It might be a good idea to play along like you're still with the plan until we find where he really stands."

"You keep surprising me. How did you know about him?" Abrego asked.

"The three Che Guevaras? Isn't it obvious?"

"Yes. I guess it is."

"But what can we do now?" Narez asked. "We don't know if they can hear us, even here."

"If there's a broadcast mike you couldn't find, it has to be very small, which means it can't be direct to satellite, like the GPS responder, so it won't have a range of much more than a hundred meters or so. They can't hear you here. When you go off the wharf, be talking about how you can't figure what I know or where I stand, other than

I'm looking for Harris's killer. I asked some questions about Morales and Vega. You didn't tell me anything. You pretended to not know any Morales, and Vega was someone you met at El Critico and said hello to on the street. I'm mad as hell about someone paying Mono to steal my computer, and he claims it was just a kid who brought him a note and some money. No sense in getting him killed, even if it would be no loss to the world. Maybe this Donzo was seen talking to Mono and I want to know about him, too."

They agreed and Clint went back off the wharf. They came back toward town fifteen minutes later. Clint noted that Vega was close to the land end of the wharf. He was behind a big hibiscus bush, trying to not be seen. Clint figured there must be a bug somewhere on Abrego or Narez. He spotted Vega with his exceptional peripheral vision and acted like he didn't know he was about. He went into the little park and talked with Erika, a girl he had known for several years. Vega put a mini-earphone in his ear as soon as he thought Clint couldn't see him. Narez and Abrego came off the wharf and he slipped the earphone into his pocket and called to them. They walked toward town together.

Clint went to the station to talk with Esteban for awhile. He explained what he'd done with Abrego and Narez. Vega was probably second in command. He was sure Sara was behind it. It was probably a cell type operation. Donzo was another second in command, in Costa Rica.

"Clint, I think that perhaps Sara is second in command. The real top one is in Colombia or Venezuela. Sara and Donzo were arguing, which a second in command would not do with a first in command. Donzo, in Costa Rica, Sara, here. They were arguing about a Colombian, which could be Vega or the head person. They would argue about him, but not with him."

Clint thought that over. It was true enough.

"Then we have to make Abrego ... no. Vega. We have to make Vega do something that will make it imperative that Sara contact the bigshit jefe."

"Esteban, Donzo causes trouble here. I don't think he wold be top man in Costa Rica. I know Morales isn't."

"Donzo spends more than half of his time in Costa Rica. We've watched him, according to the records, for more than three years. He goes to Rio Sereno and into Costa Rica. He doesn't use Frontera."

"Then he's their messenger boy. We have to know who he contacts in Costa Rica."

Esteban went through a file. "He's watched by the police in Costa Rica. They think he may be a minor drug distributor. They don't say why." He flipped on the intercom and asked Gilda to come in. She came in a couple of minutes later to ask what they needed. She said she had a contact in the police in Costa Rica who may be able to tell her something, but they had to be aware that he would be the type to accept a bribe and lie.

She said to be very quiet and picked up the phone, checked a little book from her pocket, and asked for Lt. Mostas.

"Carlos? Gilda here. Panamá. We have a little problem with a man we think might be a runner. He uses Sereno."

"Hi, Gilda. Who?"

"Donzo Vinca."

"Minuto!" There was a long pause and a few sounds of file drawers opening and closing. "Hmm. Vinca. Badio, Naro, Vicente, Mario ... Donzo, real name Donaldo Flores. A watched, secondary. Not any big deal, if at all. May be just delivering messages between someone there and Paterno. Geraldo Paterno F. F is for Flores. A brother or uncle or something, maybe. These people claim to be relatives where they aren't, too many times."

"What's Paterno into?"

"Nothing. Maybe some illegal booze, but half the people around Frontera are. Booze, phony

Rolex watches, that kind of thing. Has a little finca where he raises chickens. Meets with the lower types a lot. Maybe they sell the stuff for him. Not important."

"Then drugs aren't suspected?"

"Not in any quantity, no. Never been caught with a gram on him."

"Thanks, Carlos. We were chasing the wrong man, then."

"That's what we spend half our time doing. Caio!"

She hung up. "What you needed?"

"A good part of it. It's a lever."

"I think I can use that lever," Clint said. "Does this Sara woman go anywhere?"

"She has a little restaurant in Manaca. She's there at night, most of the time," Esteban replied.

"A good place to meet people casually, without comment, no?" Gilda suggested.

"She's here in Puerto Armuelles, now. I'll have to contrive to be there as soon as she gets back. So far as I know, she won't know who I am."

They talked awhile. Gilda said she didn't think Sara would stay more than a day or two. She bought restaurant supplies in Puerto Armuelles, was about all.

Clint said he would walk around and try to run into the three Che Guevaras, by chance, somewhere.

He walked around, but didn't come across them. At about three thirty, Esteban called to say Sara had gone back home – and that Donzo's body had been found in a ditch, cut to pieces a la Harris.

"Donzo? Why would ... he.... Cripes! I still won't know who told her! They were talking about my suspecting him of something vague when they were in range of Vega's little bug!"

"Well, it would seem someone is getting very nervous!" Esteban said.

"True. Very true, but which one – or ones."

Esteban showed Clint the body. The arms and one leg and the head were alongside the rest of the corpse. There were slashes all over him.

"I'd say our killer works himself into a frenzy and goes in swinging a very sharp machete," Esteban suggested. "He will be a cool character, usually. Sort of a method actor killer."

"Esteban, can you find how many were killed like this in Costa Rica and Colombia? I think you can't get information from Venezuela."

"I think I can try. With computers, it isn't so hard to trace. I can tell Venezuela we're after the hit man for a group that wants to cause political upheaval in four or five countries by leaving very bad images of the various governments to cause uprisings. They know exactly how that works, there!"

Clint sniggered. "I think Hanrady rides again. Tonight!"

"Han ... oh. That disguise you used in Santiago when we were working together in David. That might be a very good idea. She will know who Clint Faraday is, even if she's never seen you. If she's ever seen you from any distance, she won't recognize you."

Clint slowly nodded. "I'm going to try to locate at least one of the Guevara Trio. I want to try to learn a bit more about ... anything.

"Esteban, we seem to have uncovered a plot to start a guerilla war – somewhere – by someone, somehow, and somewhen. That's a lot too much of indefinite information. We have to have one or two points cleared up or we're, as per Abrego, chasing our tails until we're dizzy. Or something as weird.

"Was Harry just a planned goat? Was Donzo? Who's the goat and who's the real bigshit?"

"How do you figure Harry as a goat?"

"Would you, as someone planning such a scheme, check up on the ability of a middleman to produce what he said he would? Would it be any harder for them to learn he was all mouth and no action? Would you consider sending anyone as obvious as the Three Guevaras as contact men?

"Something's very wrong here! Somebody's being set up. I think it's us!"

Esteban considered, then nodded. "So! We go along like we suspect nothing, but covering our tailfeathers all the way!"

"We're flying blind – or whatever cliche you like – in this."

"So! We were flying visually blind, but our radar has discovered something!"

"Sheesh!"

They chatted awhile, then Clint went around the town for an hour, but didn't come across anyone he particularly was looking for.

Just after six o'clock, a man who looked much like Clint Faraday, except he looked a little shorter and heavier and had a mustache and wore an expensive (but noticeable) hairpiece and wore glasses, got on the David bus at the Las Olivas road. He got off in Manaca, looked around like he was lost, and went into the little restaurant across from the main road to ask if there was a hotel close. They said there was a hostel across and about a quarter kilometer toward Frontera. He said that would have to do for tonight. He would get a meal while he was in the restaurant, anyhow.

A friendly-type dark woman in her late thirties came to ask if he liked Puerto Armuelles. She saw him get off that bus.

"Oh, I was visiting a friend, maybe you know him. Hank Weston. Las Olivas. I didn't go into Puerto Armuelles. I was there once, three years ago. It was a nice enough town."

"Hank Weston? With the red hair? Irish?"

"No. Welch. He has dark hair, but it's gray now."

"Oh. I don't know him, then. The only Hank I know is Irish, with red hair.

"Here on business?"

"Yes, but not my business. A friend in Gualaca, another gringo, wants to buy a lot of land on the Pacific and was told about Las Olivas. I know Hank and said I'd check it out."

"That big stretch where the disco was?"

"Just there to the bay between there and Puerto Armuelles."

"Will he buy it?"

"I won't recommend it until they get the ROP certified. It's too risky, as it stands."

"You look like someone in Armuelles. Do you have any relatives there?"

"No. The only relative I have in Panamá is named Faraday. He lives in Bocas del Toro, though. Not around here."

"That's who it was! Clint Faraday! He's in Armuelles now!"

"I thought he was married and has a baby and is living part of the time on the comarca. We don't keep in touch."

"He was with his wife and baby, but they went back to Bocas, or somewhere. He's working with the police here on something. A murder. Some gringo who was doing some things that he ran his mouth about and he got cut to pieces. He could identify someone we, er, or something. Now another one was cut up, the same way. I think he could identify the head of a gang of crooks and one of them shut him up."

Clint laughed. "That's him! I hear he's almost famous in some places because of his work with the police."

"Almost is an understatement. I met him and talked to him a number of times here. I noticed the resemblance. Brother?"

"No. Second cousins. Is the corvina good here? I've had some that was very good, but have also had some that was very bad."

"Er, yes. It's better than most, I'm proud to say."

"I'll have that. Patacones and ensalada. Chicha piña-naranja.

"Clinton was sort of the black sheep, in the United States. I'm glad he's straightened his life around. I've heard he's gone native, all the way, so don't know why he's in the police part."

"Yes. He was declared Ngobe by their counsel. Not only has he gone native, he's got a passport that says he's an Indigeno."

He laughed again. "*That* is Clinton Faraday, all the way!" She knew one hell of a lot about Clint Faraday. He was glad he did this. It made it more obvious he was being set up, but what for?

They chatted a little more, then she went back to

her seat at the counter, where she collected for the meals.

Clint was just leaving when Abrego, Narez and Vega walked in. They saw Clint standing there and Vega stared. Abrego said something and Narez shook his head.

They studiously avoided seeming to know Sara until she came to sit with them. She told them something he couldn't hear, except "... second cousin who says ... sheep of the ... Indigeno!"

She sat and started talking in a very low voice, but intensely. Clint left and went to the hostel. In the morning, he went back to the restaurant. Sara wasn't there. He walked around for a little while, then caught the bus to Frontera, changed back to Clint Faraday, and caught the next bus to Puerto Armuelles. The bus stopped in Manaca and Vega got on. He came to sit next to Clint to ask if he knew his cousin was in Manaca.

"My cousin? Who ... oh. Hanrady. What was he doing there?"

"Buying some land, or something."

"Oh. We don't see each other much."

"You went to Costa Rica?"

"No. I met a friend who was there. We went to some clubs. She went on to David and I'm going back to Armuelles."

They talked about the places they were passing

through until Puerto Armuelles. Vega got off just by the river. Clint went on into town and to the police station. He talked with Esteban awhile, explaining that Sara was even bigger than they thought and she knew about Clint Faraday in detail. She also knew a lot about other people.

"The Guevara Trio weren't in town last night," Esteban said. "Gilda says they took the Frontera bus, but didn't get there."

"They were in the restaurant. Vega came back on the same bus with me. They were very cozy with Sara when I left them."

"All of them?"

"All of them. We still don't know who's the goat, or for what!"

"I wonder if we ever will."

Gilda came in to say Abrego and Narez had booked a flight to Bogota from David. The flight left at ten tomorrow morning. They booked from Frontera. They had met a man in Frontera and had talked for a few minutes. Some man named Geraldo Paterno Flores.

Clint grinned. "We know a lot more by that! Did Paterno then go to Manaca?"

"It's possible. He caught the Armuelles bus. It was only a few minutes ago. He may get off in Manaca. If so, I'll get it immediately."

She got it six minutes later. He got off in

Manaca. Clint thought and asked if there was a way to raid that restaurant while he was there or anything.

"We can do an ID check of anyone not local. We do that, at times, because so many people are smuggling cigarettes ... give me a minute."

She went to talk on the radio with the person following Paterno. She came back to say, "He came to Frontera on the bus and didn't carry any luggage. He had a briefcase when he got on the Armuelles bus and was carrying it when he went into the restaurant. We can do an ID check on him because he was carrying a case that could have a stolen computer in it. That's another thing that gets carried across a lot."

Esteban nodded. She said, "Check him! Fast!" into the radio.

They waited. Seven minutes later she was told the case disappeared, somewhere. He didn't have it anymore.

"It's in that restaurant! Is Sara there?" Clint asked.

"She's been called and is coming over."

"Then the case is behind the counter or somewhere. The cook or waitress has it."

Gilda talked into the radio a few seconds and said, "We observed him carrying the case into the restaurant is why he was being checked. Produce it or you arrest everyone there. Wait until the dueña gets there."

They waited another ten minutes. The radio announced the dueña was there and the place was closed for a search. Sara tried to leave, but they detained her. Paterno tried to give the officer a hundred dollar bill to be looking the other way for one minute. He took the hundred as evidence that he was offered a bribe. Paterno was going to jail for six months for that, if for nothing else!

Four minutes later they found the briefcase in the kitchen, in the trash barrel, covered with garbage. It had a combination lock.

"Break it if he won't open it!" Gilda ordered.

A minute later she said, "How much?"

A minute later she turned to Esteban. "The case contains more than a million and a half dollars in hundred dollar bills."

"You know what?" Clint asked. "I think they found their weapons!"

"And now we will find them! We'll also find who is behind the whole thing!" Esteban said.

Clint thought a minute more, then said, "They blew it! Paterno and Sara are the goats! This is what we were being set up for!

"Esteban, do not allow Vega and company to leave Panamá!"

"How do you figure?"

"That bit on the wharf gives them away. If that was real, they would never have gone to Manaca together.

"My friend, we were manipulated by experts! If one little slip hadn't been made, it would have worked."

"What was that?" Gilda asked.

"Paterno came across the border checkpoint carrying nothing. He met Abrego and Narez in Frontera and suddenly had the briefcase."

"I see! He couldn't have been bringing the money. He got it when he met with Abrego and Narez, therefore, one of them is the real head of this! Right?"

"Nope!"

"But ... now I don't get it again."

"Would the real head of the plot be around when this went down?"

"They were on their way to David to catch a plane – which would be too suspicious!" Gilda said. "It's Vega?"

"Vega is number two. It's ... who, Clint?"

"Who's left?"

"Samuél Costas," Gilda said.

"Morales," Esteban said.

"They are the second level. They can tell us who and where the top gun is. He won't be in this country or Costa Rica. He'll be ... I'll be damned!"

"What?"

"Morales and Costas can't be touched, but they'll never make another move of any kind without it being noted," Clint said. "I don't think we can tag the real head of this for anything, unless we can break Vega down as to who paid him to kill Donzo and Harris.

"Who's the one we have now that we can't hold for any reason? Who do we only have what are known to be crooks can testify against, and that for nothing?"

"Pick up Vega! Now!" Esteban ordered. Gilda was already on the radio.

"Okay. What?" Esteban demanded.

"Something she said. '... we, er, or something.' It leaves who the 'we' could have been. 'We' includes 'me,' wouldn't you say? She also said Donzo could identify the head of a bunch of crooks and he ended up cut to pieces the same way.

"How did she know about Donzo? You kept that very quiet."

"Is that enough?" Gilda asked.

"She said that to a cop, me," Clint answered. "I can show you the official papers that say I am acting as a police officer in Panamá when I went to see Morales. If Vega breaks down and admits she ordered Donzo's death, there is only one who could be the head honcho. Honcha."

"Then we have to break Vega down," Esteban declared, positively. "How can we manage that?"

"Show him he was set up by her to be the goat. He'll go into his rage act and go after her. He can't get to her with a machete, so he'll cut her up in another way."

"He won't. Nothing to gain," Gilda pointed out.

"If he'll simply be deported if he gives her to us?" Clint suggested. "Remember, I'm known for that kind of deal. If he won't, he goes down the hard way for heinous murder."

"It's what we have. It works, or we don't get her," Gilda said. "I'd say to try. It would be a matter of making it appear she was trying to throw him to the fish for bait."

"You screwed that one up bigtime, but I agree," Esteban said.

They waited until Vega was brought in. He was acting completely confused. Clint smirked and told him to have a seat. They had some serious matters to discuss.

"Such as?" Vega asked.

"Such as the fact she's throwing you to the wolves to protect her own sorry ass!" Clint fired back at him.

There was a silence, then he said, "You have to

explain that."

"Why, I only said to shut them up, not to *kill* them!" Gilda said, sounding very much like Sara.

"Please!" Esteban demanded. "Do not tell him anything more! How can we be sure he's being truthful if you tell him what we already know?"

"Sorry. I do *not* like the, excuse the term, lady."

"What do you want? What's in it for me?"

"A deal," Clint replied.

"Deal?" Vega asked.

"You killed two people we can prove, under orders from her. We want her and for you to be sent out of this country to avoid having to house and feed you for the rest of your life," Esteban answered. "If you won't deal, you stay here and she gets to dance away to sucker in some other idiot in the same kind of thing.

"We think we know what it's about. We just want the details and to be able to tag her ass for it. We don't want this kind of thing here."

"She said that I...?"

"We knew that. We didn't have the proof," Clint said, quickly. "If you can testify, truthfully, about her involvement, we can turn it around on her. You get to go home, she gets to spend the rest of her sorry life at our expense. It's your decision.

"I want to know a few things about Abrego and Narez, but it's stuff I can dig up myself, if I have to."

"They were just being used to set up an arms buy. I think they figured that it couldn't work, that we were all being used. They told me what you said on the wharf. Abrego, in particular, was affected. He said it was true. I suspect it is."

"I suspect she also figured it wouldn't work and wanted out. Trouble is, she'd find another plot that would make her money or make her powerful or something and she would sucker others into it. She can feel safe because she can throw you to us and we'd never be able to figure out where any of it came from." Esteban said.

"She figured it that way. She had me silence the two who could show she was the person involved as designer of the plan. She is dealing with some people in Argentina, who want to start more trouble in Colombia and Venezuela to distract from what they are planning."

Clint was barely able to not show a reaction to that! Argentina?

"Argentina. Yes," Esteban said, just able to hide his own shock. "The economic thing."

"Yes. They want precedence over Brazil, but that won't ever happen. Abrego and Narez were very active about resisting the present governments in Colombia and Venezuela. I think they felt they could become Castros and become dictators, themselves. The chance of that is zero.

"She was only trying to broker an arms agreement that would leave her very wealthy. Harris had made promises that he couldn't keep, but he knew he was dealing with her, alone. He could show she was the only real criminal. She had me shut him up. It is why she recruited me when she was in Colombia and she was meeting with the people from Argentina. I had done a job for them. I had done one other before for one of them. It paid more than I thought, at the time, had ever been printed! More than five thousand dollars, US! Eighty thousand pesos! Cash!

"It was drug money. I learned that later, but it established my price. I was able to do it because a man attacked my mother when I was twelve and I had a machete, so I cut him up. I can now picture that with whoever as the man and can do the same. I don't remember actually doing it. I am there, scared and angry, then I am there, dizzy and with a body all cut to pieces.

"She was planning on getting a regular system of weapons sales going, where she would make many millions.

"Narez met her in Medellin. She saw his look, so much like Che Guevara, and knew he was a revolutionary. She told him she could get him automatic weapons if he could get the money. She worked with some people in her family in Nicaragua and Costa Rica to find someone who could produce the weapons. They came up with Harris, she made the deals with Abrego and

Narez, Harris came and we found he didn't know anyone anywhere and he couldn't produce an air rifle, much less any automatic weapons.

"Morales, a man in Costa Rica, who found Harris, said he found the real deal and could get the weapons. She had me get rid of Harris and they were going to make the deal with the man, an Arab or a Jew, who would sell them whatever weapons they could afford.

"Donzo had heard her telling me what to do and about the money Abrego was bringing for the weapons. It was time for the exchange and you were there, watching all of us.

"Donzo was handled, then you found out about the money and caught her. She probably can't figure out how.

"Abrego and Narez have returned to Venezuela, by now, I would think. The weapons will be delivered. Narez and Abrego will have them, but no longer believe the plan can work, so I would think they will sell the weapons to make their money back. Abrego is smart. He says he can get the government in Venezuela to give him the money and they get the guns. He can get into politics as a sort of semi-hero for thwarting a revolution. He knows it could never work.

"That's all I know. I would like to know how you knew about the money exchange?"

"A police officer was talking to her in the restaurant. She made a couple of statements that didn't make much sense. Abrego and Narez came in with you. You came back here and they went on to Frontera. Because of her statements, Abrego and Narez were followed," Clint said, then saw a big hole in the story. "They didn't have the money then, of course. They would have given it to Sara and gone on. They had the agreement and got the money delivered there in Frontera, passed it to Paterno, and went on down to Venezuela." He made that part up, but it was logical. Vega nodded. Clint looked at Gilda and tried to say something with his eyes she didn't catch, so he continued. "I suppose Abrego and Narez are on their way home. That's probably good for this country, and we're not really involved, beyond the murders."

She caught on and slipped out. She would cancel orders to hold Abrego and Narez.

"What you told us is very close to what we figured," Esteban said. "With what we already had and your statement of declaration, we can charge her with responsibility for two heinous murders, though they weren't."

"They weren't?" Clint asked.

"The victims weren't tortured. They were cut up after the first blow, and the first blow was fatal.

You can't torture a dead body."

Gilda slipped back into the room and nodded almost imperceptibly to Clint.

"Gilda, order the holding of Sara Bailleras for two counts of murder. Have Paterno expelled as an undesirable person. Arrange for deportation, without fanfare, of Sr. Vega, after certifying his statement.

"Well, Clint! How about a little lunch? It's about that time, and I haven't had anything today.

"Sr. Vega, would you care to join us while Gilda has your declaration printed up?"

They went out and to Yola's for the almuerza, then back to the station for the official signing and witnessing of the declaration.

Clint went to Rafael's house, packed his things, and headed for the bus. He wanted to get to his wife and child. Enough of this international silly intrigues and murders!

He was getting on the bus when Esteban came to say, "Clint! Could you wait a little? I have to talk to you about some strange people who are up to something."

He didn't need to think about that one!

"No!"

Esteban laughed. "It was a joke. Have a nice trip!"

Clint gave him the finger and got on the bus.

C. D. Moulton's works are available on most major outlets as printed or e-books. CD writes the CD Grimes, PI, mysteries, the Det. Lt. Nick Storie mysteries, the Clint Faraday mysteries, the Flight of the Maita science fiction series, books on orchid culture and many others of many types. Mystery, adventure, intrigue, science fiction, humor, fantasy, paranormal, mild erotica, and factual.